When I Talk to God, I Talk About You

BY CHRISSY METZ & BRADLEY COLLINS
ILLUSTRATED BY LISA FIELDS

FLAMINGO BOOKS

FLAMINGO BOOKS
An imprint of Penguin Random House LLC, New York

First published in the United States of America by Flamingo Books,
an imprint of Penguin Random House LLC, 2023

Copyright © 2023 by 350 Degrees, Inc. and Erlebnisse, LLC.

Visit us online at penguinrandomhouse.com.

Library of Congress Cataloging-in-Publication Data is available.

Manufactured in Italy

ISBN 9780593525241

1 3 5 7 9 10 8 6 4 2

LEG

Design by Opal Roengchai
Text set in Big Caslon
The illustrations were created by mixed media consisting of pencil and digital art.

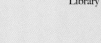

To the dreamers who love with their whole hearts

—C. M. and B. C.

For my love and my best friend, Tyler

—L. F.

When I talk to God, guess what I do?
It's really quite simple: I talk about you.

I prayed for the day that you would arrive.
I dreamt of your smile and the color of your eyes.

You're sprouting like a weed kissed by the sun.
I love hearing your giggles. You're so silly and fun.

When I talk to God,
I talk about you . . .

Making first friends and learning to share,
showing your kindness and saying you care.
You're such a great helper and the best listener, too,
always thinking of others and what you can do.

I'm proud of how brave you're learning to be.
You can do anything if you believe.

When I talk to God,
I talk about you . . .

Some days you're calm, taking things slow . . .

Some days you run. On your mark, get set, go!

There are days you'll
have questions,
some big, some small,
a hope, or a wish,
there's a plan for us all.

When I talk to God,
I talk about you . . .

But did you know
that YOU can talk
to God, too?

Your prayers are heard day or night.
God's by your side, a warm, safe light.

Pray God guides you in all that you do,
and blesses the ones who love you, too.

Tonight as you sleep, so cozy and still,
God hears your prayers and always will.

You're my sweetest prayer, a dream come true.
You're held in love and made from it, too.

When I talk to God, I talk about you.